SKY

LITTLE TIGER
An imprint of Little Tiger Press Limited
1 Coda Studios, 189 Munster Road,
London SW6 6AW

Imported into the EEA by Penguin Random House Ireland,
Morrison Chambers, 32 Nassau Street, Dublin D02 YH68

www.littletiger.co.uk

First published in Great Britain 2021
This paperback edition published 2023

ISBN: 978-1-78895-658-1

The Forest Stewardship Council® (FSC®) is a global, not-for-profit organization
dedicated to the promotion of responsible forest management worldwide. FSC
defines standards based on agreed principles for responsible forest stewardship that
are supported by environmental, social, and economic stakeholders. To learn more,
visit www.fsc.org

2 4 6 8 10 9 7 5 3

Holly Webb

SKY

Illustrated by Jo Anne Davies

LiTTLE TiGER

LONDON

For Ollie

~ HOLLY WEBB

Chapter
ONE

Lara peered out of the train window, watching the dark wild hills pass by. The journey had been exciting to start with, but now she was sick of being cooped up and starting to feel a bit grumpy. She hadn't slept well either – the top bunk in the sleeper compartment had been nearly as big as her bed at home, but the train rattled and bumped and shook, and she'd kept waking up. Lara was sure her mum had struggled to sleep too. She looked even paler than usual, and there were huge purply shadows under her eyes.

"Are you OK?" Lara asked, turning back from the window, her voice gruff. She hated asking – what would she do if Mum said no? Lara's mum had been ill for a while, nearly a whole year, but she was getting a lot better. Sometimes Lara found it hard to believe that she was really recovering.

Mum smiled at her, and then at Dad, who whipped round to stare at her, his face frightened. "I'm fine! Honestly." She patted Dad's hand, and then reached over the table to hold Lara's hand too. "The train was a bit noisy, wasn't it? But I still think it was a good idea of yours to take the sleeper, Steve. It's lovely to get the journey done overnight, and not to have to sit in the car for hours and hours. We'll be at the station in about forty-five minutes, I think. Enough time for you to finish off that breakfast, Lara."

Lara nodded, picking at her croissant. She was looking forward to seeing Gran and Grandad – it was ages since they'd last visited, and video calls just weren't the same as the real thing. You couldn't hug through a screen. Her grandparents lived in a cottage in the Highlands of Scotland, almost as far away as you could get and still be in Britain. It was at least a ten-hour journey in the car, and usually Mum and Dad and Lara drove there in the summer holidays. Mum hadn't been up to it this summer, so they hadn't been to visit for a year and a half. It seemed like forever.

"I'll go and make sure everything's packed away in our sleeping cabins," Dad said. "Back in a minute."

"I'm so excited we're having Christmas at Fir Cottage," Mum told Lara, as Dad headed off between the seats. "I loved Christmas there when I was growing up – with that huge fireplace to sit around, it's a house that's perfect for winter. It's magical. Your gran told me they've had a bit of snow already, and there's more forecast!"

Lara brightened up. A proper snowy Christmas would be brilliant, and she'd never been to Scotland in the winter before. There was even a ski resort not far from her grandparents' cottage. Except … the best bit about snow was getting to meet up with friends and have snowball fights, or make snow angels. She and her friend Anisha had made amazing balls of coloured ice when it was really cold last winter – they'd filled balloons with water and food colouring, and left pink ice bubbles all over Anisha's front garden.

Anisha hadn't said much when Lara explained she was going to be away for most of the Christmas holidays, but she'd looked so disappointed. Lara hadn't had much time to spend with her friends over the last few months – it had been so tricky, fitting in everything round Mum's hospital appointments. Lara felt like she'd spent days in waiting rooms. And when they had been at home, Mum had been too tired to have people round. Now she was getting better, Lara had been hoping for a Christmassy sleepover…

Still … Lara wanted so much for her mum to be happy. Happy and well. She could do stuff with Anisha when they got back home, there would be a couple of days before school started again.

"Is that snow up there on those hills?" she asked, pressing her nose against the train window.

"Yes, oh, look!" Mum's voice was high and squeaky with delight. "Oh, Lara, I'm so glad we're here, it's a real treat for me. And there are so many lovely things we can do. We can visit the reindeer again, do you remember doing that last time we were here? It'll be even better in the snow! And Dad says he'll take you to the ski slopes."

Lara looked back at Mum, and saw how her eyes were sparkling. Suddenly, she didn't mind being away from home at Christmas at all.

As they stepped down from the train with all the cases, Gran came hurrying across the platform to seize Mum in a hug, and Grandad scooped Lara up and swung her around. Lara couldn't stop laughing, swept away with all the happiness and excitement.

"Oh, we've got so much to tell you," Gran said, as they began to pick everything up and head through the station to the car. "All the lovely things we've got planned. And you'll never guess what your grandad saw yesterday, Lara. Something so special."

For a tiny moment, Lara wondered if Gran meant something magical – little elves, perhaps, peering in between the trees that surrounded the cottage, or a snow spirit, dancing down out of the sky. Then she smiled at herself for being silly. It was Mum talking about how special the cottage was that had done it. And the sight of snow! Now they were stepping out of the station doors, she could see the sky properly – grey and heavy and snow-laden, with a few tiny, lazy snowflakes fluttering down.

"Oh, it's snowing!" she cried, gazing up at the thick clouds.

"Yes, and there's going to be a whole lot more of it, I promise you that," Grandad said, as he pulled out the car keys. "But you still haven't guessed, Lara. What do you think I saw?"

"A pine marten?" Lara asked hopefully. Grandad had emailed her a video of a pine marten on their garden bird table a few weeks before, a gorgeous dark-furred little creature, and she really wanted to see one for herself.

"Oh…" Grandad waved the keys around as though pine martens were nothing. "He's back every other day, Lara, he'd probably steal your breakfast toast out of your hand if you let him. No, something much more exciting than that."

"I give up," Lara said, smiling at him. She could see he was desperate to tell her.

Grandad drew himself up very straight and said, in a deep, impressive voice. "A ... snowy ... owl!"

"Oh…" Lara nodded politely. She wasn't really as interested in birds as she was in other animals. And she couldn't help feeling that owls were a bit spooky.

"They're incredibly rare!" Grandad told her, looking slightly disappointed. "You only see them – oh, once every few years. They usually live in the Arctic, you see."

"What, like polar bears?" Lara asked, surprised. That was a bit more special.

"Exactly! They used to nest in Scotland sometimes, but there hasn't been a breeding pair here for nearly fifty years, and that was on Fetlar, one of the Shetland Isles. They're very occasional winter visitors here in the Cairngorms these days. I've only ever seen one once before, and that was years ago."

"Ian, we need to get in the car," Gran said, in a very patient voice. "It's cold. And Marie needs to stay warm, remember."

"Oh! Yes." Grandad unlocked the car. "I'll tell you more about snowy owls once we're home, Lara. You'll be very excited."

Dad grinned at Lara and nudged her with his elbow. "I don't think you've got any choice."

Back at the cottage, Gran led Lara up to a tiny little room right up under the roof, the one she always slept in. There was a steep, narrow staircase just for her, and it opened straight out into the bedroom. The ceiling sloped right down to the floor and there was a tiny window that looked out on to the garden – which was already flecked with patches of snow.

"Unpack your things in here," Gran said, showing Lara a chest of drawers. "And then come and have some hot chocolate. I got some of those little marshmallows you like. And that squirty cream."

Lara hurriedly shoved her clothes into the drawers, pulled on her fleecy slippers, and raced back down the staircase.

She could smell the chocolate, and a faint scent of woodsmoke – Grandad was lighting the fire.

Down in the living room, Grandad patted the sofa next to him and held up his phone. "Your mum and dad are still unpacking. Look, I've got a photo of the snowy owl to show you. It's a bit blurry, though – I was so surprised to see her. I think my hands were shaking!"

Lara snuggled up beside him and smiled gratefully as Gran passed her a mug of hot chocolate. She sniffed the sweet steam rising from it, and looked at Grandad's phone. Gazing back at her from a snow-topped rock was a huge white bird, its feathers striped and barred with black. The owl's yellow eyes were narrowed and it seemed to be glaring at Lara out of the phone.

"Oh!" Lara felt her fingers tighten around the mug. "It's so big! It looks – sort of angry, Grandad."

Grandad chuckled. "I know what you mean. I don't think she was angry. She was just keeping an eye on me, making sure I wasn't dangerous. They can be very fierce birds, though, if someone threatens their nests. Look at the size of her claws."

"Where did you see her?" Lara asked, frowning at the rock in the photo. It looked familiar. She was sure she'd climbed on it. Her grandparents' cottage nestled against a hill, and was surrounded by heather and rocky crags and patches of fir trees. Lara loved to go scrambling around the rocks when she came to stay.

"Practically in the garden!" Grandad said delightedly. "I was going up to the Big House to have a chat with Geoff – my friend who's one of the gardeners there. You met him last time you were here, Lara, but you probably don't remember. I was just wandering along the path, not paying all that much attention. I almost walked past her! But I had a feeling someone was watching me. I looked round and there she was! Perched on the rock and eyeing me up." He shook his head. "She must have come from so far away. Maybe even all the way from the Arctic, imagine that! We're so lucky."

"You keep saying she, but how do you know?"

"Well, I had to do some research," Grandad explained. "I'm not absolutely sure, but apparently male snowy owls have whiter feathers than females, and you can see this one has quite a lot of black stripes. A male owl would be white all over." He put his arm round Lara's shoulders. "I know you're probably tired from the journey, but perhaps we could go out this afternoon and try to find her?"

Grandad was looking at Lara so hopefully that she couldn't let him down, even though she still thought the owl was a bit scary-looking.

"Definitely. This afternoon."

Chapter
TWO

"This is amazing. I've never seen the cottage in the snow before." Lara walked down the path, loving the crunch of the thin snow under her boots. Then she glanced up at her grandad shyly. "I missed coming here this summer. It was nice when you came down to see us, and spend time with Mum in the hospital, but I was sad not to see the cottage … and … and all this." She waved a hand at the mountains rising around them. She didn't know how to describe the specialness of the place. "You and Gran, you belong here. It's part of you."

Grandad smiled down at her, looking surprised. "That might be one of the nicest things anyone's ever said to me," he murmured. "I wish you felt as if you belonged here too."

"Maybe a little bit," Lara said doubtfully. "Oh! That's the rock from your photo, where the owl was before!"

"Yes." Grandad slowed his pace. "I suppose it's not very likely she'll be in the same place again, but you never know."

They both scanned the rock eagerly, but there was nothing there, and Lara sighed. "Actually, Grandad – it's daytime. Don't owls only come out at night? Why was she even awake when you saw her?"

Grandad shook his head. "Snowy owls are a bit different. They often come out in the daytime. They come from the Arctic Circle, remember – the Land of the Midnight Sun. If they couldn't hunt in the daylight they'd starve."

Lara clutched at his arm and pointed. "Grandad, look – over there! Something moved – is that her? In the grass?"

Grandad went still and then he whispered, "Yes! Well spotted, Lara!"

The owl was watching them carefully between the grass stems, her mottled feathers fading into the strange shadowed snow-light. Lara would never have spotted her if she hadn't done one of those slow owl head-turns to stare at them. She didn't seem nearly as fierce as she had in the photo, Lara thought. Her yellow eyes were wide and rather surprised, as though she hadn't expected anyone to walk by.

"Are we scaring her?" Lara breathed.

"I don't know... We won't go any

closer," Grandad said quietly.

Lara nodded, gazing at the owl, fascinated. She hadn't been very excited when Grandad talked about her, but now... She couldn't take her eyes off that great white bird huddled in the snowy grass. And she was surprised by how big it was – up to Lara's knees at least, maybe even a bit taller.

As they watched, the owl seemed to gather herself up, launching into the air with a great, powerful sweep of wings. She wasn't scared at all, Lara thought suddenly. She was so strong, and so beautiful.

"Her wings are enormous!" she said, gripping even tighter on to Grandad's sleeve as the owl beat a flight across the path and skimmed the dark fir trees.

"Oh, look at her legs! It's like she's got furry trousers on!"

Grandad snorted with laughter.

"What? She does!" Lara looked at him indignantly – instead of skinny bird legs, the snowy owl really did look as if she was wearing fluffy, lacy white trousers.

"I know, you're right, she does. I got a couple of good photos of her this time. I'll send them to the local paper." He leaned down and hugged Lara tight. "Ah, that was so special, Lara. That's a once in a lifetime sighting."

"I wonder where she went…" Lara said, looking up over the trees. And she added in her head, *I wonder if we'll ever see her again.*

The next morning, Lara woke up to find that she'd pulled her duvet up over her head in the night – it was *really* cold. Much colder than it had been back home in London, she was sure. There wasn't a radiator up in the little attic room, and Gran had warned her that it might get a bit chilly. Lara pushed back the duvet and shivered. Her room was still half dark, and she reached out to the chair where she'd left her clothes, pulling on a hoodie over her pyjamas. She wriggled her feet into her fleecy slippers, and padded over to the window to look out. Yes! The slice of garden that she could see from the tiny window was thickly covered in snow now. There had been a heavy fall overnight and the garden had smoothed out to a vague landscape of bumps and curves.

"Oh, you're awake!" Her mum looked round the door, smiling. "I was coming up to tell you about the snow."

"It looks really deep!"

Mum nodded. "Your gran reckons the road might be closed if any more snow falls. It's a good thing we got here yesterday. But don't worry," she added quickly. "Gran's got so much food in the kitchen, we're not going to run out of anything. It might mean we have to put off going over to see the reindeer though."

Lara pressed her nose against the window glass. "I don't mind. I just want to play in the snow! I wish Anisha could see this."

Mum dropped a kiss on the top of her head. "Maybe it's snowing in London too. Gran's cooking a huge breakfast right now, so I'd get dressed."

Lara was too excited to eat much. She couldn't help standing up every so often to look out of the kitchen window at the garden. The change from yesterday seemed magical – it was completely different, white and bare and clean, with just a scattering of tiny bird footprints here and there.

"Can I go out?" Lara asked hopefully, as soon as she'd forced down some scrambled eggs and toast. She wasn't sure if she wanted to make a snowman, or throw snowballs, or just be outside in the snow, but she knew she couldn't wait any longer.

"I'll come too," Dad said, gulping the last of his coffee. "It looks amazing."

Lara put on all the outdoor things she'd brought with her – a thick fleece, her waterproof coat, gloves, scarf, hat, even fluffy welly socks. She had so many layers on that she could feel herself turning scarlet inside the warm kitchen, but as soon as she and Dad stepped out the door, they were wrapped in cold and quiet.

"Wow..." Dad breathed, turning slowly to look around the garden. "It's so quiet."

"I can't believe all this snow fell in one

night," Lara whispered back.

"Look at these tiny footprints," Dad said, crouching down to see them better. "I wonder if this is your grandad's favourite pine marten – they're pretty small. Or they could be squirrels."

Lara didn't answer – she was sneaking up behind Dad with a snowball. She just managed to squish it on top of his hat before he heard her coming. "Right! You asked for it."

They charged up and down the garden hurling snowballs, until Lara was hot and sticky even out there in the snow, and Dad was panting.

"Truce!" he gasped. "OK, I need a rest. And your trousers are soaked. I think we ought to go inside and dry off. We can come out again later and build a snowgirl, maybe."

Lara nodded breathlessly. Gran had said she was going to make mince pies that morning, and she wanted Lara to help her.

Later on after lunch, Lara borrowed Mum's laptop to email Anisha – she wanted to tell her about the snow, and the snowy owl too. She was planning to send her one of Grandad's photos. But when she opened her email, she saw that Anisha had already sent her a message.

I wish you were here! I'm really missing you. It's started to snow here a bit and I wish we could build an igloo like we planned. Hope you are having a good time in Scotland. Love Anisha xx

All of a sudden, Lara felt so lonely. They'd hoped to do all those fun things, and now she and Anisha were at opposite ends of the country. She didn't know what to say back to her best friend either. *I miss you too* didn't really seem enough.

Lara closed the laptop and sighed. Dad had suggested making a snowgirl earlier on, and Grandma had asked if she wanted to help make the casserole for dinner, but Lara didn't feel like doing either of those.

She was feeling grumpy and hard done

by, and she quite wanted to stomp around and tell everyone so, except she knew she couldn't, not without upsetting Mum, and Grandma and Grandad, and probably Dad as well.

"Have you finished your email?" Mum asked. "That was quick."

"Um ... yeah," Lara murmured. "Mum, can I go out again? Not just in the garden – can I go for a walk? If I stay close?" She knew that her mum had explored all over the paths and hills around the cottage when she was growing up. She had always told Lara how wonderful it was, walking in the hills by herself, or sometimes with friends from the other cottages close by. She'd said it was one of the sad things about living in London – she worried about letting Lara explore their neighbourhood on her own.

Mum looked doubtfully out of the window at the thick snow. "I suppose…" she murmured. "But you'll have to be very careful, Lara. Stay close and stick to the paths – if you can see where they are. Or maybe this isn't such a good idea. I'm just thinking that it would be easy to trip over if the snow was covering up rocks, or a dip in the ground. I should go with you."

"No!" Lara shook her head fiercely, and Mum looked surprised. "I – I just want some time by myself for a little while. Please." Lara bit her lip. She hadn't meant to say anything like that – she'd been trying not to upset Mum.

Mum frowned at her worriedly, but then she nodded. Lara wondered if maybe her mum understood more about her feelings than she let on.

"OK. If you promise to be back by, mmm, three? And you have to take my phone, just in case you get stuck somewhere. You don't know the paths and everything looks different with the snow anyway. Don't go any further than the Big House either, Lara."

"Thanks, Mum." Lara jumped up to hug her, and then went to pick up her gloves and scarf and hat – she'd put them to dry by the fire, and they were stiff and crispy with heat. Her boots still felt a bit damp inside, but she didn't mind.

Suddenly all she wanted was to be out there, running along the paths and kicking up bright sprays of snow.

Lara stood on the doorstep, gazing out into the cold. The snow had covered everything in great sheets of white, stretching all the way up to the hills and the heavy grey sky. Lara felt like shouting out into all that emptiness, but she knew that Grandad and Mum were hovering in the living room, watching her, so she tramped quickly away along the lane outside the cottage, looking back every so often at her footprints in the snow.

Mum had been right to insist on her taking the phone, she realized, as she headed down the lane. All the familiar landmarks had been smoothed away and it would be easy to get lost.

Still, she could always work out where she was by looking for the Big House, Lara thought. That was what Mum and Gran and Grandad called Firs Lodge, the huge old house tucked in between the hills. A long time ago it had belonged to a family, the Allans, but now it was a grand hotel. The estate manager had originally lived at Gran and Grandad's cottage, but bits of the land had been sold off over the years. The hotel was too big to miss, Lara was sure, and it would be all lit up. She'd definitely be able to see it.

She felt a bit better once she'd thought that, and she stopped trying to remember exactly which clump of fir trees she'd passed, or where there was a sharp rock scar poking out above the snow. This was the lane she'd walked along with Grandad yesterday, she reminded herself. She knew it well enough – and she could still just see footprints from where Grandad had been out that morning to the village shop to buy a newspaper. They made a trail for her to follow.

Lara tried to walk quickly to stay warm, but the hills and the quiet snow made her thoughtful. She found herself dawdling along, remembering. It had been such a strange year. All that worry about Mum – all that time sitting in waiting rooms and hospital wards. Mum's cancer was in remission now, and everyone was hopeful, but it was hard for Lara to let go of how scared she'd been. She shivered suddenly and realized that she'd stopped walking. She was just standing there, gazing at nothing.

The snowy landscape seemed very empty. Grandad's footprints and the soft glow of the hotel lights through the trees were the only signs of life. Lara couldn't even hear any birds calling. They were probably all huddled up somewhere trying to keep warm, she thought. So when she saw the beginnings of a snowman sticking up out of a snowy bank at the side of the lane, she stomped over, curious to see who else was around.

The snowman moved.

Lara let out a muffled yelp, and the snowman glared at her suspiciously, with round glowing golden eyes.

The owl!

Lara fumbled in her pocket for Mum's phone, wanting to take a photo to show Grandad, but her fingers were chilly and slow inside her thick gloves, and she couldn't press the power button in time.

The owl lifted her wings and launched away into the sky, leaving Lara beaming to herself as she spotted the feathery trousers again. But this time, the owl drifted down to land on a fence post a little further down the lane and she looked back at Lara, almost as if she was encouraging her to follow. Her dappled grey-and-white feathers blurred into the thick drifts and the heavy grey clouds behind her, so that she seemed almost part of the snow and the sky.

"Sky would be a good name for an owl," Lara whispered. "You belong in the sky, don't you? Please stay still, Sky. I really want to take a picture of you. Just stay there for me." She hurried on, shuffling through the snow – and the owl beat her wings lazily and swooped away, flying low between the trees this time. Lara stumbled after her, giggling. It was like a game. Sky wanted her to follow, Lara was almost sure. Or why would she keep on stopping and peering back? She would have flown away properly, wouldn't she? Lara blundered on into the shadows between the trees, following the great white bird.

Chapter
THREE

Lara glanced around a little anxiously. She wanted to keep following the snowy owl, but she was still cautious about getting lost. The light was starting to fade too, there were blue shadows pooling among the trees, and it felt colder. But when Sky swooped away this time, Lara realized she was heading towards the Big House – she could see the golden light of the windows spilling out across the snow.

Lara hurried after the white owl, stumbling through the snow to the edge of the trees. Then she stopped, drawn up short by her first glimpse of the house. She'd seen it before of course, but in summer, never like this, decorated for Christmas. There were garlands of evergreens twirling around the edges of the steps, and a holly wreath on the front door, heavy with berries. In one of the front windows stood an enormous Christmas tree, lit with what must be hundreds of flickering candles. Lara had never seen real candles on a tree before – the soft glow drew her forward, so entranced that for a moment she forgot to look for Sky.

It seemed strange to have the bright tree shining in such a silent, empty world. There should be children gathered round it, Lara thought. It felt like something out of a film, or an old picture book. But the rooms she could see through the windows were entirely empty, and there was no one playing in the snowy grounds either. Lara glanced around, wondering where Sky had got to – it was odd that she'd flown so close to the hotel. But then for such a rare, wild creature, she didn't seem very shy.

There was no sign of Sky at all now – just the snow and the golden Christmas tree light. Lara sighed to herself, watching the candles shimmer. Then she blinked – what time was it? Mum had said she had to be back by three. Reluctantly, she pulled Mum's phone out of her pocket and checked the time – she only had ten minutes to get all the way back.

Lara turned and hurried through the trees, following her own footprints, skidding and sliding in her rush. She darted through the gate into the little cottage garden dead on three, and waved to her mum, who was watching for her from the window.

"You look frozen!" Grandad called, as he opened the front door. "Did you go far, Lara?"

"Mum said no further than the Big House," Lara explained. "I saw the owl again, Grandad! But I didn't get a photo of her, she kept flying away." She frowned, wondering if Mum and Grandad would understand. "But then she would stop and wait for me, every time. It was almost like she wanted me to follow her."

Grandad nodded at her eagerly, but Mum looked doubtful. "Really? I mean, she's a wild bird…"

"I know." Lara nodded. "But she led me all the way through the wood to the Big House, and then disappeared just when I got there. But I didn't mind – I was looking at the tree."

"The tree?" Grandad raised one wild white eyebrow questioningly.

"The Christmas tree in the window! I've never seen a tree with real candles on it before, it's so beautiful."

"Real candles? They were lit?" Mum put in, sounding so surprised that Lara swung round to look at her.

"Yes, there must have been hundreds of them. They shone on to the snow. You'd love it, Mum. We should go and look tomorrow."

"That's odd," Grandad said. "I can't imagine the hotel wanting lit candles on their tree – wouldn't it be a fire risk?"

Mum nodded. "I was thinking the same thing."

Lara blinked. She supposed that was true. She had been surprised as well, when she first saw the tree. But there *had* been real candles – hadn't there?

The next morning, Lara stood by the window in the living room, looking out at the snow-covered front garden. Was Sky still out there, somewhere close? Mum and Grandad had almost convinced her that there couldn't have been real candles on that beautiful tree – but only almost. Lara was sure she'd seen them, and they'd been magical. Her whole walk had felt magical.

"Mum, can I go for a walk? I really want

to look for Sky."

"The owl?" Mum looked up, smiling. "Grandad's got you hooked, hasn't he?"

"I'll make a bird-watcher of Lara yet," Grandad said, grinning. "Do you want company, Lara? Or are you after a stomp through the snow on your own again?"

Lara blinked at him. She didn't want to hurt his feelings – but Grandad leaned over and squeezed her hand. "Don't worry, love. I'm always telling your gran that everyone needs time on their own in the wild. You enjoy it."

"But take my phone and be back in an hour," Mum said firmly.

Lara nodded eagerly, hurrying to get her outdoor things on. Only a few minutes later she was outside, the tip of her nose already turning pink with cold, her boots squeaking in the snow.

This time, she hardly had to look for Sky. She walked down the lane, gazing around hopefully, and a dark dot appeared in the sky. It was so tiny that she nearly didn't notice it, but then it came closer and closer, and Lara gasped as she realized that it was the owl, sailing over the tops of the fir trees towards her. She started to run, waving and laughing a little. "I'm here!" she called. "Sky! I'm here. Were you waiting for me?"

Sky banked slowly, gliding back in the direction of the Big House, and Lara dashed after her. This time, as she ran, Lara decided she would keep watching the snowy owl, even though she wanted to look at those glimmering candles again. She had to know where Sky went. She could imagine her perching on one of those statues in front of the hotel – that would make a brilliant photo to show Grandad.

But the trees seemed to draw their branches closer together as Lara came to the edge of the wood, and she lost sight of Sky swooping above her. When she burst out on to the grass she swung round, searching eagerly for the owl, but Sky was nowhere to be seen. Lara frowned, nibbling her bottom lip. It seemed so odd that Sky had stayed close to her all the way through the wood and then disappeared – again.

The Christmas tree's candles were shining softly out on to the snow, but Lara didn't stop to look at them this time. She walked across the white lawn, turning every so often to check in all directions. Sky must be here somewhere.

There! A small mound in the snow at the corner of the house – just at the edge of the curving driveway. But the owl looked strange, as if she were lying down. It was almost as though she had crashed to the ground, Lara thought, her heart suddenly thudding. She ploughed through the snow, hurrying as fast as she could towards the pile of white feathers. Lara didn't know what she would do if Sky was hurt – call her grandad, perhaps, or find someone in the hotel to help.

But as she stumbled up to the little mound, Lara saw that the whiteness was lace, not feathers. It was a girl, collapsed on the ground, sobbing, her white dress and white-blond hair scattered with snowflakes.

"Oh... I'm sorry..." Lara stepped back, embarrassed. She would hate it if she was crying, and someone practically fell over her.

The girl didn't say anything, she just lay there, her breath hitching as she cried, and Lara felt the strangeness of the empty house in its hushed blanket wrap around her. For a moment, she thought – was this girl the owl after all? Had Sky fallen and changed into something different?

"Wh-what are you?" she whispered.

The girl rolled over, looking up at her in surprise.

"What do you mean, what am I?" she asked with a puzzled frown. Then she sat up, shuddering, and wrapped her arms around herself, as though she'd suddenly realized she was cold. Her pale hair was limp with melted snow, and her dress and dark stockings looked soaked. Lara pulled off her scarf and handed it to her, and the girl blinked at the glittery purple wool in surprise, before slowly wrapping it around her shoulders. "Thank you…" she murmured.

Lara held out her hand and the girl took it, letting Lara pull her up out of the snow.

"You must be frozen." Lara eyed her worriedly. "Are you staying here?

Shouldn't you go inside? You ought to change, your dress is soaked."

"I'm not going inside," the girl said stubbornly. She glanced up at the window with the sparkling tree and shook her head. "No." Then she looked back at Lara. "Why did you ask me what I was? That's such a strange thing to say."

"Oh…" Lara felt her cheeks flare with heat. "Well … I was following an owl. A snowy owl. You might have seen her. They're very rare."

"An owl in the daytime?" The girl frowned at her again.

"Yes, I know it's funny. Snowy owls come out in the day, they really do. Anyway, don't laugh, but I thought you were the owl…"

The pale girl pressed her hand over her

mouth, as if she was politely trying to hold her laugh back.

"It was silly. But I've seen her a few times now, and it really did seem as if she was trying to show me something. Then she disappeared, and you were there, and she was all white feathers and you've got that lacy dress on…" Lara shrugged. "It's so eerie and quiet here too, everything just felt a bit … fairy tale. As if it wouldn't be so strange to have an owl turn into a girl."

"I suppose," the girl agreed doubtfully. "Well, I promise I'm not an owl. Oh, it's too cold to stand here. I ran out without my coat on, I was so angry…" She rubbed her eyes and then grabbed Lara's hand and pulled her away from the house and into the trees.

"Where are we going?" Lara asked,

panting as the
girl dragged
her along.

"To the
grotto. It won't
be warm, but
it's better than
being outside."

Lara remembered the
grotto – Gran and Grandad had shown it
to her on one of their walks. It was a strange
little cave built out of stones and shells,
with a pool inside it and a statue of a water
nymph over a tiny waterfall.

The girl hurried her down a path
through the gardens – someone had dug it
out very neatly and piled all the snow up
in walls on either side – and then into the
grotto. "The others won't find us here," she

explained, sitting down on a stone bench by the waterfall and pulling Lara beside her. The damp cold of the stone struck straight through Lara's trousers and she shivered. But she liked this strange, sad girl, and she wanted to keep talking to her. She could put up with being cold.

"What others?"

"My cousins." The girl made a face. "I don't mind Frances and Louisa so much, but Arthur is horrid. I hate him."

"Oh…" Lara nodded. "I don't have any cousins. Or aunts and uncles."

"Lucky for you," muttered the girl.

"What's your name?" Lara asked. "Mine's Lara."

"Amelia." The girl nodded her head in a strange, rather formal sort of way. "Amelia Allan." She twisted her fingers in

Lara's purple scarf and then said, her voice a little high and squeaky, "Thank you for pretending not to see I was crying."

"Oh … well … I wouldn't like it if I was, and someone found me… I hope – I mean, I hope you're all right."

"Not really," Amelia whispered, staring down at her fingers.

"You could tell me, that is, only if you wanted to…"

Amelia glanced up at Lara, her face puzzled. "Maybe I will. I thought I didn't want to see anybody, or talk to anyone at all. But it seems different, talking to you. Perhaps it's because you're a stranger. It feels as if you don't belong. Are you from one of the cottages?"

"Yes, I'm staying with my gran and grandad. They live here and I live in

London. We came up on the train."

"Oh! That explains why you don't sound like the other children on the estate."

Lara wasn't sure what Amelia meant by that. She didn't think there were any children living in the other cottages close to Gran and Grandad's.

"We travelled on the train too. On the sleeper," Amelia went on.

"Yes. I hadn't been on a sleeper train before. It was fun to start with, but it took such a long time even though we slept for most of the journey."

"Mmm." Amelia glanced over at Lara again. She looked a little surprised, and Lara wasn't sure why. "Do your parents let you wear boys' clothes like that?"

Lara looked down at her tracksuit

bottoms and boots, and then at Amelia's lacy dress. They did look different… But she'd never heard anyone say that trousers were boys' clothes. Amelia didn't sound as though she was trying to be mean – she genuinely seemed confused. "Yes…" Lara said slowly. "I often wear trousers."

"Oh. How … unusual. They look very comfortable," Amelia added quickly. "And warm. Thank you for lending me this pretty scarf." She was silent for a moment and then she swallowed hard – Lara could see her throat moving. "I was crying because I'm sad, I suppose. Because my mother died."

"Oh!" Lara felt the words like a push, a hard jolt as if Amelia had shoved her. "Oh… I'm sorry." Should she say anything about her own mother? Would it help to say that she had been so afraid that her mum would die? But she hadn't, she'd got better. Perhaps saying that would just make Amelia feel worse.

"And it was my fault," Amelia added, scowling at Lara as though she expected her to gasp and run away.

"Oh…" Lara said again. She couldn't think of anything else to say.

"I made her come exploring on the beach with me this summer, when she was already ill. And she caught cold and died."

"Of a cold?" Lara wasn't sure that could really happen, but Amelia seemed convinced.

"Yes, and she's angry with me about it. She's haunting me."

Lara couldn't stop herself squeaking. "What? Like a ghost?"

"Not *like* a ghost. Really a ghost." Amelia shivered. "I see these strange white shapes on the landing, floating along in front of me, and horrible crying. I hate going anywhere it's dark and shadowy now. And all of this house is dark and shadowy."

Lara blinked. It was an odd way to talk

about the hotel.

"I don't believe in ghosts," she said firmly. "I don't see why your mother would want to make you scared."

"No…" Amelia looked thoughtful. "But maybe she wants to talk to me?" She slipped her hand into Lara's and Lara jumped – it was so cold.

"You should go inside! I know you don't want to, but your hands are like ice."

"I'd rather stay here," Amelia insisted. "But you're right, I should change my dress, and put my coat on. You could come and see my room while I change?" Amelia gave Lara a hopeful look and stood up, and Lara followed her slowly to the entrance of the grotto. She probably ought to head back to the cottage, but she was too curious. She'd never seen inside the hotel, for a start.

It was when Amelia led her in through a back door and past the kitchen that Lara started to think that something was wrong. The kitchen was full of people, all wearing old-fashioned clothes like Amelia's. The oven was a huge black metal range – she'd seen something like it when they visited a stately home, but no one cooked on something like that these days, did they? It certainly didn't look like a hotel kitchen.

They went up a rather dingy set of back stairs, and along a passage lined with doors. None of them had numbers, and the room that Amelia took her into clearly wasn't a hotel room. It was very clean and tidy, and the furniture was pretty, but there were scuffs and scratches on the little desk, and a mark on the carpet where someone had spilled something. There was a bookcase and a shelf of dolls.

This wasn't a hotel. And Amelia wasn't strange and out of place. Lara was.

Lara stood by the door, looking around in confusion, while Amelia pulled another long, full-skirted dress out of the wardrobe and then dashed back to her. "Could you undo my buttons? I can't reach."

What was going on? Amelia had been

talking about ghosts, but now Lara couldn't help wondering if this strange girl was a ghost herself. She had to be *something*. This wasn't right...

She isn't a ghost, Lara told herself, as she worked on the long line of little pearl buttons with slippery, fumbling fingers. *Ghosts don't have buttons. Not buttons that you can touch.*

But what is she then? Or – what am I?

Amelia was wearing the fanciest underclothes Lara had ever seen – a vest with strips of lace sewn all down the front, and then layers of lacy petticoats too. Lara supposed it meant at least Amelia hadn't been soaked through to her skin – but she couldn't imagine needing someone to help her get dressed every day.

Amelia dragged on the clean dress, but she had to get Lara to help her button it up again. Then she pulled on a fresh pair of stockings, and then a coat and a flower-trimmed hat, and hurried Lara back along the passageway. "Come on, we won't have much longer before someone comes to find me. Oh no!" She whirled round and pushed Lara towards a velvet-cushioned window seat. "Behind the curtain! Quick!" she hissed, and Lara did as she was told. Were they hiding from the awful cousin? Arthur?

"It's my governess," Amelia whispered, nodding towards the stairs. "Miss Morell."

"Amelia! Where are you? Oh, come along, Amelia!" A young woman walked along the passage past them, her long dress rustling and swishing against the floorboards. As soon as she went into the bedroom, Amelia gasped, "Now!" and raced for the stairs, with Lara dashing after her.

As they spilled out into the gardens again, Lara almost forgot the strangeness of the house. Amelia was no ghost, no one so red-faced and giggly could be. Lara pounded after her through the snow and Amelia looked back with a grin, tossing a handful of snow at her. They darted in and out of the trees, throwing snowballs and chasing each other.

Every so often Lara would think – "But
that kitchen…" or "Her clothes are so
strange…" or "Who has a *governess*?"
but she was too busy dodging snowballs
to worry about it properly. And then she
raced around a tree with a fat snowball to
catch Amelia with – and saw that she was
in the lane, right in front of the cottage
gate, and her gran was at the door, waving
at her.

Lara waved too, and then turned to look back through the trees. But there was no sign of Amelia at all.

"There you are! I was starting to think you'd got lost. Did you have a good time exploring?" Gran went to give Lara a hug as she hurried indoors, but then she laughed and stepped back when she saw how much snow Lara was wearing. She helped Lara unzip her coat instead and shook it out of the front door. Lara peeled off her gloves and hat, and draped them over a stool near the fire to dry off.

"Oh, Amelia's still –" She was about to say, *Amelia's still got my scarf*, but then she stopped herself. She had a strange feeling that if she told Gran about Amelia, a girl who lived at the Big House, Gran would smile and tell her that she must have made a mistake.

No one lived at the Big House. It was a hotel. Lara *knew* that.

But I know I didn't just lose my scarf. I can't have imagined Amelia and everything she said. She was real…

"I saw the owl again!" she said instead, forcing herself to smile at Gran.

"Oh, that's wonderful! We must tell your grandad. Ian! Lara saw the owl!"

Grandad came hurrying out of the kitchen, looking excited, and Lara's mum followed him. "Again! Did you get a photo?"

Lara showed him the photo on Mum's phone, with Sky perched on a fence and looking back at her, as though waiting for Lara to catch her up. "It was like yesterday," she explained. "Like she really wanted me to follow her. She didn't seem shy at all. And she went so close to the hotel – and then … and then … I lost her." She stumbled over her words, not sure what to say next. She couldn't say, *And then she led me back into the past, when the Allans lived in the Big House before it was a hotel.* Grandad would think she was making it up. If only she'd thought to take a photo of Amelia too – would she even have shown up in the picture?

"Don't worry!" Grandad looked delighted. "I wonder how long she's going to stay. This is so exciting. Look, Marie. Lara got so close to her!"

Lara's mum took the phone to admire the photo. "I'd love to see Sky too. Shall we all go out looking again tomorrow?"

Lara nodded slowly. Sky seemed so magical – like a key to another world. Who knew what else she might find?

Chapter
FOUR

The next morning, Lara got up early – she was downstairs even before her gran, and she opened the front door to look out at the snow. No more had fallen overnight, but it had frozen very hard and there were icicles crusted along the edge of the roof and around the porch. Lara ran her finger down one and it gleamed with meltwater as it stole the heat from her skin.

"Lara! Were you hungry for breakfast, love? Oh, shut the door, it's so cold." Gran came down the stairs, shuddering.

"I wanted to go out and look for the owl," Lara explained as she closed the door. "Grandad wasn't sure how long she was going to stay. I don't want to miss her." *And I want to find Amelia…*

Gran laughed. "He's got you hooked

too, hasn't he? He was so pleased to have something special to show you. Eat something first, at least." Then she stopped, her eye caught by something outside the kitchen window. Gran put her finger to her lips and beckoned Lara over, and Lara leaned on the sink to peer out. She could see the bird table, and a little metal table and chairs – all wearing layers of snow. Perched on the roof of the bird table and twisting down to look inside was a slim, dark-furred creature.

"The pine marten! Your pine marten, Gran!" Lara whispered delightedly. She'd almost forgotten about the rare marten, they'd been so excited about the owl. The pine marten gobbled a mouthful of seeds and then turned round to look directly at the window. Lara could see him so clearly, the creamy orange fur under his chin, even his tiny sharp teeth. He looked a bit like a small skinny bear, she decided. She giggled as the pine marten glared at her and Gran watching, grabbed a mouthful of sultanas and shot away across the snow.

"Grandad puts sultanas out for him every evening," Gran explained. "He loves them. And his other favourite food is jam. We'd put some leftover toast crusts with jam on the bird table and the pine marten thought they were best thing he'd ever tasted. So now I leave my crusts on purpose…"

Gran looked a little bit embarrassed, as if Lara might think she was spoiling the pine marten, but Lara hugged her. "Please can we have toast now? I'll definitely leave my crusts."

By the time Gran had put toast on, everyone else was downstairs too, and eager for a walk. Lara fidgeted while her mum and dad drank coffee, wishing they'd hurry up. She'd loved seeing the pine marten, but she was desperate to go back to that strange snow-world she'd slipped into the day before. She was almost certain that she needed the owl to help her find it. If she tried to walk through the woods without Sky, Lara was sure the hotel would just be a hotel.

She hurried everyone into their outdoor clothes, almost pushing Dad to get his boots on, and chivvying them out of the front door. Even though Lara couldn't stop thinking about Amelia, a little part of her was watching her mum tramp through the snow, her cheeks scarlet with cold, smiling and chatting with Gran. Mum had seemed fragile for such a long time. Now she looked herself again, and Lara loved it.

Suddenly Mum stopped, clutching Grandad's arm. "Look! Is that her?"

Grandad whipped around, lifting up his binoculars. "Oh yes, well spotted, Marie! Ah, she's off..."

The snowy owl had been sitting on a rocky outcrop, gazing at them with her lamp-like yellow eyes – now, as they watched, she swept her great wings down and launched into the air, swooping away into the trees.

"I'm going to follow her!" Lara gasped, setting off at a run. She didn't even think about what would happen if Mum and the others came too, she just wanted to find Amelia again. Lara disappeared between the pine trees before anyone could stop her, struggling to cross her fingers inside her gloves. She could hear someone calling ahead of her, she was sure. Tiny drifts of snow sifted down as she brushed against the branches, and Lara hurried on. She kept catching glimpses of Sky's barred feathers, or a flash of her bright eyes.

She could see the beautifully tended gardens of the hotel now, the fountain gently splashing, and the grass as soft and fine as a carpet.

There was no snow.

Lara stood watching, her heart thumping in a strange, slow beat. Amelia was sitting on the edge of the marble basin, dipping her fingers in the water. The sun was sending rainbows through the drops, and the air was thick with the scent of roses. The time had changed, Lara thought, biting her lip as she looked around. It felt like early summer, May or June. She was far too warm in her winter things – Amelia's dress was thin cotton, with sleeves only to the elbow. Lara tucked her hat into her pocket and unbuttoned her coat before she stepped out on to the lawn.

"Lara!" Amelia jumped up with a yelp of delight and ran to hug her. "Oh, you came back! I have your scarf – it's been folded up in paper in my wardrobe all these months! I thought I would never see you again."

"I – I had to go," Lara mumbled, hugging her back. "I'm sorry."

"Are you staying longer this time?" Amelia asked eagerly. "I missed you. Oh, I have a pony! Uncle Rory gave him to me – he used to be Arthur's but Arthur is too tall for him now, and Uncle Rory said that since I'm staying here to be with my cousins, I should have him. And he likes me better than he ever liked Arthur. Come and see."

Lara glanced behind her, wondering suddenly if Mum and Dad and Gran and

Grandad were about to spill out into the gardens – but there was no one following her.

She took Amelia's hand and Amelia led her along the gravel paths behind the house to the stables. In Lara's day, these had been made into a spa, for massages and treatments. Dad had bought Mum a manicure as one of her Christmas presents – he'd told Lara and made her promise to keep it a secret. But now there were great horses looking out over the wooden half-doors, and a boy was standing out in the yard, grooming a small white pony with a fluffy forelock hanging over his eyes.

"He's called Merlin, because of Arthur," Amelia explained. "I would have called him Snowdrop, but never mind. How is he today, Alec?" she asked the boy.

"Feisty, Miss Amelia. You watch out for him when you have your lesson this afternoon." Alec glanced curiously at Lara, obviously wondering who she was, but he didn't ask.

Amelia smiled and then dug around in the folds of the wide sash tying her dress, eventually pulling out some lumps of sugar. "I stole them from breakfast," she whispered to Lara, who was thinking that it was quite clever to hide things in a sash, but Amelia's beautiful dresses clearly needed pockets. Then again, Amelia did keep looking sideways at Lara's trousers. She obviously still thought they were odd.

"Have you heard the news, miss?" Alec asked. "Neil and I, we found an owl's nest, up on the hill. Great white ghost owls! The nest's full of eggs too."

"Ghost owls…" Amelia's eyes widened and she looked over at Lara with a shiver.

Lara squeezed her hand and smiled at Alec. "Could you tell us where the nest is? Would it upset the owls if we went to look?"

Alec shook his head slowly. "Not if you keep your distance, miss. You head up the hill, towards that old dead pine."

He pointed at the bare, rocky hillside that rose behind the house and Lara saw the tree he meant, standing alone and dark against the heather. "It's not much of a nest, just a dip in the heather. You'll see her sitting on the eggs. Watch out for her mate, though. He's off hunting most of the time, but he'll go for you if he sees you going too close to his eggs."

Lara nodded. "We will. Thank you."

The two girls set off up the hill, making for the tall, scarred pine. "You told me about the owls last time you were here," Amelia said as they scrambled around the rocks. "That's what you thought I was."

Lara nodded. "Snowy owls. I was following one." *And again today,* she added to herself. *She brings me here. I wonder why?* "Alec's right, they do look a bit like ghosts." She glanced over at Amelia, noting the pale, pinched look on her face. "Do you still see your mum – I mean – the white shapes in the passage?"

"Yes," Amelia muttered. "Not very often. But sometimes."

"The owl I saw wasn't frightening," Lara promised her. "She was beautiful. And they're very rare. It's special to see them."

"Mama would have liked that," Amelia whispered. "She loved to watch birds, and animals. She knew so much about them. She would have known about snowy owls, I'm sure."

Lara caught her sleeve. "I think I can see her! There, just by that rock."

"Oh!" Amelia gasped. "She's enormous!"

The two girls gazed at the owl, a soft mound of feathers surrounded by grass stems and heather. She was staring back at them too, her yellow eyes fierce – but Lara didn't think she was angry, just cautious. She was beautiful – and so familiar.

It couldn't be the same owl, Lara knew that. But then, Lara couldn't be here in the past either. "Sky…" she murmured, and Amelia glanced round at her.

"Is this the same owl you followed? You named her Sky?"

"I think so," Lara said slowly, watching the owl ruffle her snow-white feathers. She had the same dark markings just above her eyes that Sky did – two dark dots.

She was the same bird. She had to be. Maybe it was all right that Lara didn't understand. She would just – believe.

"Let's not go any closer," Amelia whispered. "I – I don't think she would like it."

Lara nodded. "We can watch from here. I wonder when her eggs will hatch?"

The two girls settled down in the scented heather, watching the dappled owl. After a little while, she seemed to stop worrying about them, her eyes half closing as she basked in the warm sun.

Lara was starting to feel a little sleepy too, when Sky's mate returned to the nest in a silent flurry of wings. He was white almost all over – Lara could see why Alec had called them ghost owls. He leaned protectively over his mate, offering her something small and furry – Lara thought maybe it was a rabbit, and she felt very sorry for it.

"Ugh…" Amelia made a face as the two owls ate – they were quite messy – and the male bird whipped his head up, glaring around.

"He heard me!" Amelia flinched back against Lara as the male lifted his wings and let out an angry, grunting bark. The two girls watched worriedly as Sky stretched up, nuzzling gently at her mate. He was still glaring at them, but he lowered his wings, stomping around the nest as if he were working off his bad temper.

"Maybe we should go," Lara breathed, as quietly as she could, and Amelia nodded. The two girls crept quietly backwards through the heather, stopping by a rocky outcrop to look at the owls again.

"They're both flying now," Amelia said worriedly. "We didn't scare her off the eggs, did we?"

"I don't think we can have done." Lara frowned. "She didn't look frightened. Oh! Alec said he and Neil saw the eggs. She can't sit on the nest all the time, if they saw them. Maybe she just wanted to stretch her wings."

Amelia nodded, looking relieved. They were just setting off towards the house, when they heard a scuffle and a grunt further down the hillside. Amelia pulled Lara back into the shelter of the rock, her finger pressed against her lips. They watched as a tall, blond-haired boy scrambled past, and Amelia whispered in Lara's ear, "That's Arthur!"

"Do you think he's looking for the owls too?" Lara breathed into her ear, and Amelia nodded worriedly.

"He collects eggs… He has a box of them, with labels on. He swaps them with the other boys at his boarding school."

"You mean he steals them from nests?" Lara felt her nails dig into her palms, and realized she was clenching her fists. That meant the eggs would never be able to hatch; he was taking away Sky's chance of owlets. That boy – that horrible boy who teased Amelia all the time, even when she was so sad – was not going to have the eggs. Not if she could help it.

"No," she said firmly, and Amelia looked up at her in surprise.

But then the younger girl shook her head, glaring at her cousin further up the hill. "No. But how are we going to stop him?"

Her voice wobbled a bit, and Lara realized how scared of Arthur she still was. She put her arm round Amelia's shoulders in a quick, encouraging hug. "I don't know yet. But we'd better follow him."

It had taken Arthur longer to find the nest without the dappled white owl sitting on her eggs. He was just crouching down to look greedily at them as the girls caught him up.

"Leave them alone!" Amelia cried, and Arthur glanced round at her lazily. He didn't seem the slightest bit worried about being caught.

"Why?" He smirked at her. "What are you going to do about it?"

"You shouldn't be touching them," Lara snapped. "They're rare birds!"

"I know that! Why do you think I want their eggs?" Arthur sneered.

"But there aren't many of them left! Leave them alone. And you shouldn't be stealing eggs anyway, even if they weren't rare."

"And you two are going to make me?" Arthur started to laugh, and Lara saw Amelia's face crumple.

"Yes," she hissed at him. "You're not having them!" Lara ran forward, thinking that maybe she could push him away from the nest, but then he stood up, and she realized how tall he was – how much bigger than her all over.

"Come on then," he taunted her, smirking.

Lara's stomach seemed to twist inside her. There was nothing she and Amelia could do to stop him. It was so unfair – the poor owls would come back and find all their eggs gone…

The owls! Maybe the two girls couldn't stop Arthur, but the owls could! Grandad had told her they were fierce if they were protecting their nests. Lara whirled round, catching a look of surprise on Arthur's face, and scanned the harebell-blue sky. There! One of the owls, not that far away.

"Sky!" Lara shouted. Sky had come when she called in her own time, hadn't she? "Sky! Come back!"

"What are you doing, stupid?" Arthur said, but he sounded worried, and now he was looking up at the sky too.

It did seem stupid, to think that the owls were listening to her, Lara knew that. But then she saw them – Sky and her mate, swooping down in a flurry of white. Lara darted back to Amelia and the girls scrambled away. Arthur tried to follow them, but the male owl dive-bombed him, clawing at him with furious cackles.

"Get it off me!" Arthur yelled. "Help! Get off! Ow!"

"Should we do something?" Amelia whispered. "Oh, it scratched him!"

Lara watched as Arthur fled down the hillside, pursued by the male snowy. His face was bleeding, two long red scratches marking his cheek. "It's all right, I think the owl's coming back," she told Amelia. "Arthur's far enough away now."

Sky examined her eggs anxiously and

then settled herself back on the nest. Her mate fluttered back to nuzzle at her, and Lara smiled to herself. It looked just as if they were having a conversation about their poor eggs and that horrid boy...

Amelia threw her arms around Lara and hugged her tight. "I know I shouldn't be glad the owl clawed Arthur," she whispered fiercely, "but, oh, I am!"

"Me too."

Both owls looked up, gazing at the girls, their golden eyes fiery against the white feathers. Lara tensed, wondering if the birds thought that they were threatening the nest too – but all they did was stare at her and Amelia for one quiet moment, a silent thank you.

Chapter
FIVE

"How's Arthur?" Lara asked Amelia as they climbed the hill to see the owls again during her next visit. For her it was only the next day, but a couple of weeks seemed to have gone by in Amelia's time.

Amelia put her hand across her mouth, giggling. "He's sulking. He couldn't explain what had happened to Uncle Rory and Papa, you see. My uncle is very excited about the owls – Alec had told him about them too, and Uncle Rory ordered the gamekeeper and all the estate staff not to disturb the nest. And he said the same to Arthur, but Arthur went straight off to steal the eggs! I'm sure Uncle Rory suspects what happened, but Arthur made up some silly story about getting scraped by a tree when he was on his bicycle. His face looks awful. Aunt Grace is worried it might scar."

"I'm not surprised." Lara shuddered. "Those claws were huge!"

"You were so clever to call the owls back," Amelia told her, but then her smile faded.

"What's the matter?" Lara asked.

"Oh… Nothing… I just wish that Mama had been here to see them, that's all."

Lara nodded. "You told me she loved to watch birds."

Amelia smiled. "Last summer, when we were at the beach, she was so happy. We went looking in all the rock pools, and we watched the gulls. We even saw a cormorant fishing, Mama was delighted!" She was silent for a moment, and then she added, "That was on one of her better days, when she could stay out for quite a while. Papa was cross, he said she shouldn't have risked her health." Amelia stopped walking and looked up at Lara. "But I think Papa was wrong."

"She was doing something she loved," Lara murmured. "With you."

"Yes. She was happier out on the beach than she ever would have been shut indoors." Amelia nodded, her face set in a grim, determined effort not to cry. "And I think you were right, when you said Mama wouldn't want to haunt me. She only walks along the passageway because she misses me, like I miss her. Not because she's angry! There!"

Lara squeezed her hand. "She never would be."

"When I saw her a few days ago, I didn't run away. I just stood there and watched her, even though I was scared." Amelia swallowed a gasping breath and said, "Now-let's-go-to-the-nest!" all in a rush.

Sky was still brooding over her eggs, but when the girls came close, they saw that a tiny greyish-white shape was snuggling against her at the edge of the nest scraped in the heather.

"They're hatching!" Lara breathed, her eyes bright with excitement. "Oh, look at the chick, he's like a little old man…"

The owlet was covered in a fluffy greyish-white down – nothing like the parent owls' crisp white feathers at all. As they watched, Sky leaned down and pecked at something piled around the edge of the nest. She came back up with a piece of meat in her beak, which she fed to the tiny chick – the girls could see him gulping it down greedily, and then he let out a wheezy scream for more.

"They've got a larder," Amelia said, looking fascinated. "Look, she's got food all piled up ready to feed them…"

"Her mate's coming back." Lara pointed to the male snowy, skimming low across the ground towards the nest. He settled neatly next to her, offering up another small rabbit, and the girls watched, fascinated, as she swallowed it down in one piece. Sky's mate inspected the tiny, fluffy chick – was Lara imagining that he looked proud? She wasn't sure. Then he launched away again, swooping up into the sky to carry on the hunt.

They kept on watching for a while, lying stretched out on the honey-scented heather. Sky stayed on the nest, her head turning from side to side as she scanned the hillside for dangers to her chick.

At last the two girls headed back down the hill. Amelia's cousins, Frances and Louisa, were chasing each other around the fountain, and the governess Miss Morell was sitting on the edge of the marble basin.

"Why does Arthur go to school, but you all have a governess?" Lara asked, and Amelia sighed.

"Because he's a boy. Everything's different for boys. I might go to school when I'm a little older. I'd like it, I think – Arthur gets to play cricket and he learns more interesting things than we do. Miss Morell likes watercolour painting and nature walks, and that's all very well, but not every day. Don't let her hear us, she's bound to say I should be practising the piano. Come on, let's sneak back inside before anyone notices. We can sit and talk in my room."

Amelia led Lara up the back stairs again. The house seemed strangely dim and shadowy after the bright sunlight outdoors, and Lara heard Amelia's breath start to come more quickly as they reached the dark hallway outside her bedroom.

"Are you all right?" she asked.

Amelia turned, her cheeks flushed. "It's so silly. I know I shouldn't be frightened, but I can't help it… Even if Mama isn't angry with me, I hate the thought of ghosts…"

Her hands were shaking, Lara realized. "What did you actually see?" she asked, looking around.

"A shape," Amelia explained slowly. "A pale shape, all hazy. Every time, it drifts across the corridor in front of me, and then disappears! And the house suddenly seems cold." She shivered.

"Mmm…" Lara didn't think it was cold, actually. Just not quite as warm as it was outdoors in the sun. Amelia wasn't making it up, though – she was pale and shaky, and her eyes were round with fear. Lara walked along the passage, glancing at the furniture – an old rocking horse stood against the wall between the windows, and there was a big wooden chest where the passage turned a corner.

"Where does that lead to?" Lara asked.

"Arthur's room, and Miss Morell's at the far end," Amelia explained.

Lara went to peer round the corner – just more slightly battered-looking passage with faded carpet. The downstairs rooms

were a lot grander. Then she lifted up the
heavy wooden lid of the old chest and
smiled to herself. It was mostly empty, but
there at the bottom was a piece of fabric,
thin and gauzy. She lifted it out and held it
up between her and Amelia. Underneath
it was a battered candle lantern.

"That's an old bit of muslin curtain,"
Amelia said uncertainly.

"Yes." Lara nodded. "But imagine if you put a light underneath it – like that lantern. It would be all pale and glowing and ghostly, wouldn't it? I think this is where Arthur keeps his ghost costume."

Amelia was still pale – but she was white with anger now, rather than fear. "You mean it was him all the time?"

"I think so." Lara nodded. "I don't know for certain. I've never seen a ghost and I don't think I believe in them. Maybe your mother is watching over you. But I don't think it's her you keep seeing in the passageway."

"I can't believe I fell for it…" Amelia shook her head. "Give me those. I won't let him try that on anyone else!"

"I don't think he would anyway," Lara said, handing her the cloth and the lantern.

"It worked for you because he knew you were so sad about your mother. That's such a cruel thing to do. He really is awful."

"I can't believe he's part of my family," Amelia muttered furiously. "I'm even more grateful to that owl for clawing him now. All that time…" she whispered. "All that worry. There never was a ghost." She sighed.

"Are you … disappointed?" Lara asked. At least the imaginary ghost had been a last thin connection to Amelia's mother.

Amelia shook her head slowly. "No… Mama was such a bright person. Always outdoors and dashing about. She didn't droop around in hallways. Ugh. I should never have been taken in." She bundled the muslin under one arm and grabbed Lara's hand. "Come with me?"

"Where?"

"I'm going to find Arthur and … and tell him what I think of him!"

"Try and stop me," Lara said, squeezing her hand. Amelia looked so fierce just then – she reminded Lara of Anisha, back in London. Anisha never let anyone push her around, even when she was scared. Lara wished the two of them could meet. "I'm definitely coming with you. Is he in his room?"

"I think so." Amelia swallowed hard and then marched down the passage to bang on Arthur's door.

"What?" came an unfriendly voice from the other side.

Amelia hesitated for a moment, and then she opened the door and strode in, with Lara following her. Arthur's room

was bigger than Amelia's and it was
untidy – not very untidy, since there were
maids to clean up after the children, Lara
assumed, but there were papers scattered
around, and cast-off clothes. There was
also a glass-fronted case of birds' eggs
hanging on the wall.

"What do you want?" Arthur was lying
on his bed, reading – and then he spotted
Lara's armful of muslin and smirked.
"Oh… You worked it out, did you? Took
you long enough."

"You were the ghost," Amelia said
quietly. "It was you all the time."

He nodded, still smirking. "Didn't think
you'd be stupid enough to believe it."

"She isn't stupid," Lara hissed. "She
only believed you because she misses her
mother! You're a disgusting person."

"And she's a silly baby." Arthur shrugged. "As I said. She shouldn't have been so easy to trick. It's sad, really."

Lara stared at him, hardly believing he could be so unkind. She could imagine how Amelia had felt, wishing for her mother so much, and then seeing Arthur's mean joke. She could imagine how *she* would have felt… "Amelia's lucky that she's not cruel like you," she said quietly. "You should be ashamed, thinking something like that was funny."

Amelia pulled at her arm. "Leave him, Lara. Come on. It's no use expecting him to say he's sorry, is it? We shouldn't have come."

"Yes, run away and play," Arthur sneered as the two girls walked out, both furious. "You and your strange little friend. Where did you find *her*, Amelia? The scullery?"

"Let's go. I don't want to be anywhere near him," Amelia muttered.

They wandered through the trees. Lara was trying to think of stories about school to tell Amelia, things that wouldn't seem too strange or modern. Lara was in the middle of teaching Amelia to play "A sailor went to sea, sea, sea" when Amelia dropped her hands and turned towards the lane. "Did you hear that?"

"Lara! Are you there? It's lunchtime!"

"Oh… Is that your mother calling?" Amelia said wistfully.

Lara nodded. She couldn't think what to say, but Amelia didn't seem to be sad, or jealous. She only smiled and backed away a little. "Come again soon," she whispered, and then darted off towards the house.

"I've never known you to spend so much time outside," Lara's mum said, smiling, as Lara hurried across the lane and up the cottage path. "You haven't got your gloves on, or your hat! Aren't you freezing?"

Lara shook her head, although of course it was bitterly cold now, back in the winter snow.

"So, who were you playing with?" her mum asked. "I could hear two of you singing."

Lara blinked. Mum had heard Amelia? But thinking about it, Amelia had been the one who heard Mum calling her first.

"She's someone staying at the Big House," Lara explained. She could feel herself smiling, so much that Mum laughed, and hugged her. Somehow it made Amelia and the owls even more special, knowing that her mum was a part of the story too.

Chapter
SIX

"What did he say?" Lara asked. Lara was back with Amelia again, and in Amelia's time a few days had passed. It was still the heat of summer, and Lara had thrown off her winter coat as soon as Sky led her out of the trees. Amelia was sheltering in the cool of the grotto with a book, but she'd jumped up as soon as Lara arrived, eager to tell her about Arthur's latest nastiness.

"He's been watching us – he said he's seen us going up to the owl nest, and he said that…" She went pink. "I don't think this, Lara, not at all, it's what *he* said…"

"Something about me?" Lara asked, her fists clenching.

"He said I was keeping low company with servants' children, and that he was going to tell my papa. I don't think he has, though. Papa doesn't like Arthur very much either, he thinks he's spoilt."

"He is!" Lara agreed. And a snob too. Lara had already worked out that the people who lived in the cottages in Amelia's time mostly worked on the estate, and a rich landowner's niece like Amelia wouldn't usually be friends with their children. She thought it said good things about Amelia that she didn't care.

Arthur was obviously different. Part of Lara wanted to storm up to the house and say that, but she was glad Arthur hadn't told Amelia's father about her, or his own father. They would probably know who lived on the estate better than Amelia did. Her father would wonder who this strange girl was, who kept appearing and disappearing. She frowned, thinking over Amelia's story. "If Arthur's seen us going up to the nest, does that mean he's watching the owls too?"

Amelia nodded. "I think so. He said something about all the eggs being hatched now – there are four chicks!" Her face lit up, but then she frowned. "I don't trust him, Lara. What if he does something to hurt them? He's still angry about the owl clawing his face." She glanced out of the doorway of the grotto. "I know it's hot, but shall we walk up the hill? Just to make sure the chicks are safe? The one who hatched first looks so big now!"

When they reached the nest, Lara tried to count the owlets, but it was difficult to see them buried under Sky's feathers. "I can only see small ones," she whispered to Amelia, and Amelia nodded. She was looking around anxiously.

"Oh! There, look!" She pointed, and Lara narrowed her eyes. Amelia was pointing at grass, and heather… Then she saw a pair of worried orange eyes gazing back at her, and a tiny beak in a face full of fluff. But the chick was much bigger than when she'd last visited. It must be at least half the size of its parents, she thought.

"What's it doing over there?" she murmured to Amelia. "Shouldn't it be with its mother?"

"I don't know," Amelia whispered back. "Maybe the big chick won't fit in the nest any more. It's very well hidden in all those grasses. Perhaps it's trying to stay away from foxes?" She made a face. "Or people like Arthur."

Just then the male snowy landed

between the girls and the nest, and Lara caught her breath. She hadn't even seen him coming, he was so silent. Then she pressed her hand over her mouth to hold back a laugh as another plump grey chick suddenly erupted out of the heather, hopping across the ground and flapping its tiny wings in excitement. The chick the girls had been watching set off at a speedy waddle as well.

"I don't think they're lost," Amelia whispered, and Lara nodded.

"The father seemed to know where it was, didn't he? It does look as if they're hiding on purpose, to keep themselves safe. I hadn't spotted the other one at all. I wonder how far away from the nest they go?"

When the male snowy swooped away again, the chick who had been fed settled down in the heather, looking rather smug. The slightly smaller chick who'd missed out set off back to the nest, obviously hoping that Sky would have something to feed it on.

"Are you thirsty?" Amelia asked. "I'm still hot after walking up the hill. We could go and paddle in the burn, and get some water to drink."

"Let's," Lara agreed. Her feet were far too hot in her wellies, and splashing about in a stream sounded wonderful. They circled away from the nest, not wanting to upset Sky and the chicks, and followed the noise of the water gurgling over the stones. Lara loved the little streams that threaded through the stony ground here and she'd missed playing about in the water – back in the winter of her own time, all the streams were frozen and buried under snow.

They were sitting with their feet in the water, and Lara was rubbing her toes over the smooth pebbles when Amelia suddenly laughed. "Skip! What are you doing here? Is Uncle Rory with you?"

Lara looked up and saw she was talking to a beautiful liver and white spaniel, who had appeared on the other side of the tiny stream and was watching them curiously.

"Here, Skip," Amelia called, holding out her hand coaxingly. "Uncle Rory must be somewhere close by, Skip is always with him."

"He's lovely," Lara said admiringly. "So spotty."

Skip had obviously decided that Lara was safe enough – he splashed across the stream to lick Amelia's hand and then shake himself over the two girls. Then he plunged out of the water and on to the bank, jumping about excitedly and chasing the bees buzzing in the heather.

"You silly dog." Amelia shook her head at him. "You'll get stung – don't eat them, Skip!"

But Skip had stopped chasing the bees

now. Instead he was frozen still, one paw raised and his tail twitching wildly. He looked so excited.

"What's he seen?" Amelia asked, clambering up out of the stream. "Is it a rabbit? No, Skip! Leave it!"

Skip wasn't listening – he was too fascinated with what he'd found. He darted closer, nudging at something with his nose, and then jumping back in surprise as whatever it was hissed loudly. Lara climbed up after Amelia, hoping that Skip hadn't disturbed a snake – Mum told her she'd seen an adder once, sunning itself at the edge of a path.

The hissing was followed by an angry clicking noise and a rustle of wings, and Lara gasped. "It's one of the chicks!"

"Skip, leave!" Amelia yelled. "No!"

But Skip was far too interested to back away. He kept running at the little owl, darting in and out, and barking. Amelia tried to grab his collar and pull him away, but he was too strong for her.

The owlet was clicking its beak and spreading out its wings to make itself look bigger, but it wasn't scaring Skip. The dog seemed to be getting more and more excited, and he was starting to snap at the chick now too.

"He'll hurt it!" Lara said anxiously. "We have to stop him!"

"I haven't got anything to tempt him with," Amelia panted, as she tried to reach for Skip's collar again. "Uncle Rory gives him bits of biscuit sometimes. Oh, where *is* Uncle Rory?"

"I've got biscuits!" Lara said, digging into her trouser pocket. Gran had given her a little packet of mini cookies when she'd gone out on her walk, to keep Lara going, she said. Lara pulled the packet apart, nearly spilling them into the long grass. "Skip, here, look! Biscuits!"

"He's not listening." Amelia stopped trying to catch Skip, and shoved him away from the owlet instead. "Biscuits! Go to Lara!"

The spaniel seemed to catch the smell of the treat, and he glanced round at Lara hopefully – but then he looked back at the owl chick, obviously thinking that this bouncing, fluffy thing was even better than biscuits. The chick hissed at him again, but more faintly this time. It was getting tired, Lara thought.

"No!" Amelia snapped. "You're not having it!" All at once she crouched down next to the chick and pulled the skirt of her white pinafore over it, hiding the owlet from the excited dog.

Lara gasped – the owlet might look fluffy and sweet, but its beak and talons were terribly sharp. She wasn't sure she would have been as brave as Amelia. The chick clicked its beak again, but then it fell silent, muffled under the fabric.

Skip backed away a couple of steps and barked, obviously confused, and Lara tipped half the little biscuits out into her hand and shoved them under his nose.

"Good boy," she murmured. "Nice biscuits. Come on…" She backed away from Amelia and the chick, feeding the biscuits to Skip one at a time and tempting him back across the stream.

"Skip! Here, boy!" A man's voice was calling from further down the hill, and Skip's ears twitched. He gobbled the last of the biscuits out of Lara's hand and disappeared off at a run, heading towards Amelia's uncle. Lara leaped back over the stream.

"Are you all right?" she called to Amelia.

Amelia nodded. "Thank goodness you had those biscuits. I don't think Skip would have given up if you hadn't tempted him away."

Lara crouched down next to her. "Is the chick hurt? Did it claw you?"

Amelia pulled her pinafore back, revealing a ruffled and furious-looking owl underneath. "Only my pinafore," she said, showing Lara a long set of slashes in the material. "I don't think it's hurt," she added, looking worriedly at the owlet.

The chick glared back at her and clacked its beak loudly, as if to say it had been very badly treated. Then it waddled away, swiftly disappearing into the long grass.

"You were so brave!" Lara told Amelia, crouching down to hug her. "I would have been far too scared to do that."

Amelia blushed scarlet, but she looked delighted and she hugged Lara back.

"I knew Mama would have done something," she said slowly, as if she was thinking it out for herself. "She'd never have let Skip hurt the baby. I had to be like Mama."

Chapter
SEVEN

Lara looked round at the sea of presents and wrapping paper, wondering how her mum and dad had managed to sneak it all into their luggage. She was sure they couldn't have had room for any clothes.

"Do you like the art set?" Mum asked hopefully, and Lara beamed at her.

"It's brilliant." She had wanted new paints for ages, and now she had a whole set with a paintbox, pencils, everything. She couldn't wait to try doing a painting of Sky and the chicks.

That was the one sad thing about it being Christmas Day. It meant they were halfway through their stay, and it wouldn't be long until they were going home. Time had felt strange and slow all through the holiday, since Lara had been spending all those summer days with Amelia and the owls, but now another week seemed nothing at all. At first Lara had been glad they weren't staying in Scotland for the whole of the Christmas holidays, but now she wished she had longer. She didn't mind that the deep snow had meant that they couldn't go on all the trips that Mum and Dad had planned, either. She'd spent her days in another world instead, in another time. It was too hard to think she might never see Sky again – or Amelia.

Lara was planning to look for Sky that afternoon – she'd promised to help Gran make the Christmas dinner and she couldn't just disappear and leave her family on Christmas morning. Dad had suggested a family walk later on, to help work off the Christmas pudding, but it was hard to feel the time she had to spend with Amelia and the owls ticking away.

They were just setting the table, when her dad glanced out of the window and whistled. "Look at that! The snow's really coming down again. Not sure we're going to be able to have a walk after all."

Lara went to the window and stared out anxiously. "I like walking in the snow," she said hopefully to Dad, but he frowned.

"Not sure it's a good idea, Lara. Look how thickly it's falling."

"You wouldn't be able to see your nose in front of your face," Grandad said,

146

patting her shoulder. "Were you wanting to go out looking for the owl again? I expect she'll be huddled up sheltering from the wind and the snow somewhere. She won't want to be out and about in a blizzard."

"Perhaps we can all watch a Christmas film this afternoon, instead?" Dad suggested.

Lara nodded, but she couldn't help feeling disappointed. Only a few more days left…

"I don't know whether I'll be able to see you again," Lara said quietly.

A week had passed, and she and Amelia had climbed the hill to watch the owlets stretching out their wings. They were starting to look a lot more like Sky and her mate now, with masks of white feathers around their eyes, and the two oldest chicks had speckled wing feathers like their mother's. They were a strange mixture, mostly black and white feathers, but still with a chick's soft grey down around their heads.

Lara was sure that the older ones would be able to fly any day now. They were practising all the time, running over the heather and flapping wildly. Every time they tried, they seemed to get a little further off the ground, but then after a few seconds they would bump back down on to the heather again, looking disappointed.

The two girls were sitting on a rock, not far from the owls' nest, sharing a piece of Christmas cake that Lara had hidden in her coat pocket. She looked round at Amelia and saw her face fall. "We're going home tomorrow night on the sleeper – to London."

"But you'll come back?" Amelia asked. "You'll come to stay with your grandparents, won't you? You went away before."

"Yes…" Lara stared down at the crumbs of cake on her palm, not sure what to say. How much did Amelia understand about her strange comings and goings? Lara was sure she must have realized something was different about her. "I want to. I love it here, and it feels so different this holiday, as if I almost belong. But I still might not be back for a while. It's a long way. And even if I'm at the cottage, I don't know if I'll be able to visit *you*." She threw the crumbs on to the grass, and sighed. "You know it isn't just that I walk down the lane, don't you?"

Amelia nodded slowly. "The owl. I don't understand it, but that first time, you said you followed her here. She's something to do with it, isn't she? And when you come here, you never seem to know what day it is, or what the weather's going to be like. You're always dressed for winter…"

"It's winter at home," Lara said, her voice cracking a little bit.

"I told you I didn't believe in ghosts," Amelia murmured. She stretched out a hand and cautiously patted Lara's arm. "I really don't, not any more. You aren't a ghost. I know you can't be, ghosts aren't solid.

But you're not one of the Lovell family who live at the cottage, or even a relative of theirs from London. You're … something odd. One of the Sith, maybe. You know, magical people. Fairies. Miss Morell told us about them."

"I'm not. I promise that I'm just as real as you are," Lara said sadly. "I wish I could keep on coming back. I hope I will! But I think I can only get here if I follow Sky."

Amelia said nothing, and Lara stopped twisting her fingers together and made an effort to meet the younger girl's eyes. "Oh, please don't look like that! I didn't want you to be frightened of me, that's why I didn't say anything."

Amelia nodded, but she slipped down from the rock and brushed the cake crumbs off her pinafore. "I have to go. Miss Morell will be looking for me."

"Please don't!" Lara called. "It's my last day!" But Amelia was already disappearing off down the hill.

"Goodbye, Amelia…" Lara whispered. Then she swallowed hard and looked over at Sky, settled calmly on her nest.

"What am I going to do?" she asked, but the white owl only gazed back at her, yellow-gold eyes shining.

Lara shifted uneasily in her sleep, muttering to herself and sighing – and then she sat up in bed with a start, her eyes wide open and her heart thumping.

There had been a noise. Something odd had woken her, something out of place.

There it was again. A soft thud against her window. Lara clutched the bedcovers tightly, peering into the darkness. The noise was eerie. She wanted to pull the covers over her head and pretend she hadn't heard. But what if the thing that had thumped against her window came to find her? That would be even worse, just waiting for it to arrive.

Lara climbed out of bed, wrapping the

covers around her shoulders like a cloak, and padded cautiously to the window. The noise came again, and she gulped with fright – but then she heard another sound, faint and whispery. A worried voice calling from down below. "Lara! Lara!"

It sounded like Amelia, she was sure, but how could it be? Amelia had never found her way into Lara's time, it had always been the other way round.

Lara shoved hard at the stiffly iced window, pushing it open at last, and craned her neck to look down into the dark garden. There was a small figure out there, hard to see in the golden light of a lantern. "What are you doing?" she called to Amelia. "You walked over here on your own, in the dark?"

"I've got a lantern. And I wasn't on my own – I followed her." Amelia turned, holding the lantern up so that Lara could see a tall, pale owl, perched silently on top of the wall around the garden. "I need your help, Lara! Please come!"

"I'm on my way," Lara called. "Just wait there." She inched her door open cautiously, listening for Mum or Dad or her grandparents, hoping they hadn't woken up. But everything seemed quiet in the cottage.

Lara crept downstairs, trying to tread as softly as she could. Then she felt her way across the kitchen with her hands out, trying not to bump into things, and fumbled at the lock on the back door.

"You're here!" Amelia clutched at her gratefully as she pulled the door open.

"What is it? What's the matter?" Lara wasn't sure whether to be excited or scared – after Amelia had run away from her that afternoon, she'd thought they would never see each other again, but something was obviously very wrong. Her friend looked so frightened, and there were tear tracks shining on her face in the lantern light.

"It's Arthur. He's going to shoot the owls!"

"What? He can't!" Lara gasped.

"Yes, he can! He has a gun. Uncle Rory gave it to him last Christmas. We have to go, come on, please. I'll explain on the way."

"Wait here a sec." Lara crept quickly out to the hallway to grab her coat and boots. She also grabbed Grandad's big torch from the shelf by the door, just in case.

Then she hurried back to the kitchen and pulled the door closed after her, following Amelia through the shadowy garden. Both of them flinched in surprise as Sky swooped low over their heads and disappeared into the night.

"What's going on?" Lara demanded.

"I overheard Arthur talking to Frances. That's about the only thing that's nice about him, he does love his little sister, even though he teases her all the time. She was crying in the garden because she'd lost her doll's best hat, and Arthur told her not to worry, he would get her some beautiful feathers to dress a new hat with. White feathers, he said! He was going to go hunting specially for her, in the middle of the night, and he'd bring her some beautiful white and speckled feathers!" Amelia brushed her hand across her face to wipe tears away again, and sniffed. "He's never forgiven Sky's mate for scratching his face. He must have been thinking about it for ages, and now Frances has given him a reason to go after them."

"But I thought you said your uncle didn't want the owls hurt?" Lara pointed out.

"I know. I suppose that's why Arthur's going at night. He said to Frances that it was a secret, and she mustn't tell. He didn't know I was sitting in the grotto with my sewing." She looked worriedly back at Lara. "I didn't know what to do, or how to stop him! I thought of telling Uncle Rory, but he wouldn't believe me. He wouldn't *want* to believe me. So I decided to go up the hill to try and keep watch over the nest, but when I crept out of the door by the kitchens, Sky was there, waiting for me. She was perched on the iron bracket for the bell pull. She frightened me so much, I nearly screamed. But I knew I had to follow her, even though…" Her voice trailed away and Lara sighed.

"Even though you didn't want to. Are you frightened of *me*?"

Amelia held her lantern up to look close into Lara's face. "No," she said at last, sounding quite surprised. "No, I'm not. Although … the cottage… It doesn't look the way it should. The kitchen's different…" She shivered. "I'm out of my time, aren't I?"

"Maybe…" Lara admitted.

Amelia wrapped her cloak tighter and walked on. She called back over her shoulder. "I don't know what you are, or how I'm here, Lara, but we need you now."

Chapter
EIGHT

Lara had been out in the dark before, of course. But never in the middle of the night, and so far away from people. The night seemed to belong to the creatures rustling through the grass and calling from the trees. She and Amelia were trespassing.

"I didn't think it would be so dark," Amelia muttered, stumbling as her foot slipped on a pebble.

"I know," Lara whispered back. They seemed to be moving in a tiny bubble of light, cast by the lantern. The blackness pressed in around them, thick and velvety. "Are we close? I can't tell. Everything looks so different."

"That's the big rock that's close to the nest, I think…" Amelia murmured. "Oh!" She reached out to clutch at Lara as a low, rasping hoot sounded just in front of them, followed by Sky clacking her beak.

"She heard us," Lara said. "We came to help!" she called.

There was a shuffle of feathers and the two girls saw Sky's eyes glowing in the lantern light. She stopped clacking and settled back on to the nest.

"I think she trusts us," Amelia said. "Lara, how are we going to help them? It's all very well guarding the nest, but I think Arthur will just keep trying."

"Shhh…" Lara whispered. "Is that someone coming?"

There were definitely footsteps – then a rattle of tiny stones and a muttered curse.

"It's him!" Amelia looked around wildly. "What shall we do?"

Lara thought for a moment, then she pulled Amelia back against the rock. "Put your cloak over the lantern," she breathed. "Don't let him see us. Listen, if we wait for him to get a bit closer, then you can slip behind him to the path. Fetch your uncle! If Arthur's out here with a gun, he'll have to believe you."

"But what are *you* going to do? I can't leave you here, and we've only one lantern!"

"I've got a lantern of my own, look." Lara pulled the torch out of her coat pocket and flicked it on, shining the beam across the snow and making Amelia gasp. "I'll be fine, and I've got an idea. Go, Amelia! We need your uncle to catch him in the act."

Amelia looked uncertain, but at last

she nodded. "Are you sure you'll be all right?"

"Yes! Hurry!"

Lara watched her creep away behind the rock, and shivered. The night seemed much colder, and darker, now that she was alone on the hillside with Arthur.

And the owls, Lara told herself. *Sky came to fetch Amelia because they needed us. I'm not really on my own.*

She turned off the torch again and then she leaned against the rock, watching Arthur's lantern bobbing around as he tried to search for the nest, and waiting for him to get close enough. He kept stumbling about, nowhere near the nest, and Lara wondered for a moment if they were making too much fuss. Arthur didn't look as though he'd make a very good hunter. But then again, he only had to be lucky, and the owlets still couldn't fly away. They had to distract him somehow.

Amelia had given her the idea, when she'd wondered if Lara was a fairy person, one of the Sith. Gran and Grandad had taken her to visit some caves a year or so ago, and Lara had bought a book of Scottish legends in the gift shop. It had been full of tales of fairies and kelpies and the Ghillie Dhu. They were known for tempting travellers off the path, tricking them into bogs and quicksand, or leading them away into fairy worlds. Lara didn't think Arthur would truly believe in fairies, but out here in the middle of the night she hoped that she could convince him for just long enough. It would serve him

right for trying to frighten
Amelia with his mean
ghost trick.

Lara held her
fingers over the
torch so that
only a tiny chink
of light shone
between them.
Then she slipped
out from behind
the rock and walked
as lightly as she could
over the grass, right in front
of the tall boy.

"What…" Arthur stopped dead.
"Who's there?"

Lara didn't answer. She swallowed, and
licked her lips nervously, and then she

began to whistle. In the dark of the night, Arthur would see a faint dancing light, and hear an eerie music. Lara wasn't very good at whistling, but she didn't want Arthur to recognize the tune anyway.

Arthur muttered something under his breath, and then he said again, "Who's there?" But his voice was higher, and squeakier. She'd scared him! Lara sucked in a breath and then tiptoed closer, whispering a stream of nonsense words.

"Stop it! Go away!" Arthur said, his voice shaking – and then Lara nearly gave it all away as Sky floated low and silent overheard. The owl was so close that her wings seemed to brush their faces. Lara swallowed her scream, but Arthur yelled, dropped his lantern, and blundered away down the hill.

"It worked," Lara whispered gleefully to herself, but then she nibbled her bottom lip. She hadn't actually meant to scare him that well – they wanted him up on the hillside for his father to catch. Still... Perhaps she and Sky had put him off for a while, at least?

Lara followed Arthur, treading as quietly as she could. She could hear him skidding and scrambling about, so it was easy enough to stay out of his way.

"There he is! I told you!"

Lara stopped dead and quickly put out the torch. Amelia had done it! She'd brought her uncle up the hill in time.

"Arthur! What are you doing out here? I didn't believe your cousin when she told me. I trusted you!"

"There's something up there!" Arthur flung himself forward, grabbing at his father's sleeve. "I heard something – and there was a light!"

"What on earth are you wittering about, boy? Give me that gun and get back to the house. Amelia, where are you? Come along, child."

"I'm coming, Uncle," Amelia called, but she hurried up the path towards Lara instead and Lara went to meet her.

"What did you do?" Amelia asked delightedly.

"Pretended I really was one of the fairy folk." Lara smiled at her. "But I'm not."

"I know… Goodbye, Lara. You will come back if you can, won't you?"

"Yes, I promise. Now you should go, your uncle's calling. Keep watch over the owls for me!"

Amelia nodded, and then darted away after her uncle and her cousin, leaving Lara standing alone on the hillside, her eyes filling with tears. Amelia was gone, and tomorrow she was leaving.

A low hoot sounded close beside her and Lara sniffed, raising up the lantern. Sky was there, perched on a rock, her speckled-snow feathers gleaming in the light, ready to take Lara home. The owl hooted again as she launched herself into the night, and Lara knew she was calling her to follow.

"Lara, wake up, darling. You need to finish off your packing. Remember we're going out to see the reindeer before we catch the train."

Lara blinked, and stared at her mum. For a moment she wasn't sure where she was – or when she was. But her bed was covered in a flowery duvet, and she was wearing her Christmas pyjamas.

"You look so sleepy!" Mum laughed. "Come downstairs, Gran's made a huge breakfast for our last day, everyone's favourite things."

When Mum had gone, Lara sat up in bed, wrapping her arms around her knees and trying to remember what had really happened the night before. It felt like a dream – but then so did all her time with Amelia and the owls.

"We did it…" she told herself. "We kept them safe." She ought to be happy, but she kept thinking, *I wish I could go back…*

Lara got up slowly, shivering as she pushed her feet into her slippers, and pulled on a thick sweater over her pyjamas. She leaned over to straighten out the duvet and stopped, staring down at her pillow.

On it was a feather. A white feather, faintly marked with bars of black. Lara reached out to pick it up, turning it lovingly between her fingers, knowing that somehow Sky had left it for her to find.

As the train began to pick up speed, Lara pressed her nose against the window. It was hard to see Gran and Grandad in the glare of the reflected lights, but she knew they were there on the platform, waving one last goodbye.

Lara looked down at the little wooden box in her lap. Grandad had given it to

her when she showed him the feather —
he said she needed somewhere special to
keep it safe. Lara hugged it tight, smiling
to herself. If she brought it with her
when she came again next summer, then
perhaps Amelia would be waiting for her?

She could hope, at least.

Far above the hurrying train, a great
white owl swooped, calling into the night.

Turn the page for an extract from

One brave cub.
One extraordinary escape.

LUNA

From MULTI-MILLION bestselling author

Holly Webb

Hannah turned round slowly. It was like being inside a huge snow globe, she thought. Or maybe a music box. Everywhere she looked there were sparkling lights and Christmas trees. The air was filled with a rich, spicy, gingery smell. It was full of snow now too, the flakes twirling down lazily to settle on the cold pavements. Hannah had never seen anything so magical. She pulled up the furry hood of her parka round her neck and shivered happily.

"What do you think we should do first?" Mum asked, squeezing her hand. "I can't believe it's started to snow. It's just perfect!"

"I want to go on that, Mum!" Hannah's sister Olivia said, pointing at the huge Ferris wheel glittering above the square.

"It's so big!"

"But it's snowing!" Hannah pointed out.

"Actually, I think it's a great idea," Dad said. "That way we'll get to see all of the market and we'll know what there is to do. And it isn't snowing much, Hannah, just a few flakes. I don't think it'll stop us seeing the view."

Hannah nibbled her bottom lip doubtfully. The wheel really was very big. It was moving now, twirling slowly round, and the red-painted seats looked wobbly. She wasn't sure she wanted to be all the way up there. But Olivia was dancing about excitedly, desperate to dash across the square and join the queue. Olivia was two years younger than she was. If her little sister was brave enough to go on the wheel, Hannah wasn't going to admit she was scared.

She did sit huddled up close against Mum, though, when they finally got into the little carriage. Dad was sitting opposite, with his arm round Olivia's waist, holding on to her tight. She was so keen to see everything that she wanted to lean right out over the edge.

"Are you OK?" Mum whispered as the wheel gave a lurch and their carriage started to rise slowly in the air, swinging back and forth.

"Yes," Hannah squeaked. "It's just… It's just high."

"I know. I'm a bit nervous about it too. Olivia takes after your dad. He always wants to go on those big rides, doesn't he?"

Hannah nodded. It made her feel a bit better that Mum was scared as well. Better enough to lean sideways a little and peer at the market below. She hadn't realized how big it was until now. The huge square was filled with hundreds of stalls and sideshows, all lit up with glittering lights. The *Striezelmarkt* was the biggest of the Christmas markets in Dresden but there were lots of others – they spread out all across the city. Since they were only there for a couple of days, Mum and Dad had said they should come to this market first, since it was the oldest – maybe even the first Christmas market there had ever been.

There had been a market here in the square since 1434, nearly six hundred years in the past. Of course, the city had changed a lot since then. Mum and Dad had explained that during the Second World War, the British had bombed Dresden very heavily and hardly any of the old buildings were left. It had made Hannah feel strange to hear that. She'd known about London being bombed in the war but she hadn't thought about the bombs her own country had dropped.

"Oh, there's a carousel," Hannah said,

pointing. She could just make out the horses galloping under the stripey roof. The carousel music threaded faintly through the air towards them, over the rattle of the wheel and the chattering crowd. "And there's a … I don't know what it is. There, look." They stared down at the glittering tower below. "Is it another carousel? There's figures on it but I can't see anyone riding on them, though."

Dad leaned over to look too. "Oh, I know this one! It's a Christmas pyramid." He scrunched up his nose, frowning. "Let me see if I can get this right. A *weihnachtspyramide*. They're very traditional. People here have been making them for years. They have a fan at the top – those blades, can you see? Like a ceiling fan. You light candles underneath.

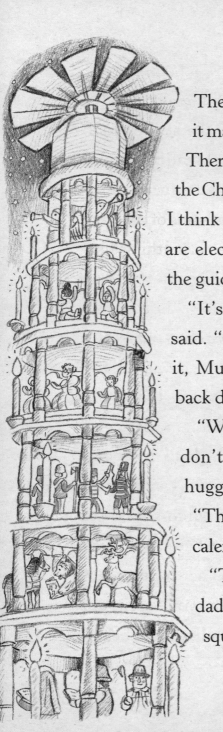

Then when the hot air rises it makes the fan spin round. There's always a giant one at the Christmas market, though I think the candles on this one are electric. I read about it in the guide book."

"It's so pretty," Hannah said. "Can we go and look at it, Mum? The wheel's going back down now."

"We'll look at everything, don't worry!" Mum said, hugging her and laughing. "The tree, the giant advent calendar."

"The ice rink," Hannah's dad put in, and Olivia squeaked with excitement.

"Yes, yes! Can we go skating now?"

"Later on. There's a place close by where they have a huge Christmas tree right in the middle of the ice rink," Dad said. "Let's go and look at some of the stalls first and then we can see everything else. Maybe we could get some gingerbread?" He helped Hannah and Olivia off the metal steps and then sniffed loudly, making them laugh. "I can smell all those spices and I'm starting to feel hungry."

They wandered along the pathways between the wooden stalls. Each one was like a little hut and the shiny red roofs were slowly disappearing under a layer of snow. There was so much to look at that Hannah knew she'd never be able to see it all. She kept turning round to gaze up at the pyramid above them and the enormous

Christmas tree, which was even taller than the Ferris wheel. Dad bought cups of hot chocolate and Hannah thought it was far nicer than any chocolate she'd had at home. There was a sweet, spicy taste to it – or maybe it was the snowflakes landing on the whipped cream top that made it so delicious.

Mum wanted to get some Christmas decorations, so she kept stopping to look at the stalls. But there were so many that Hannah didn't see how she was going to choose.

"Oh, look," Mum said, stopping at a display of brightly painted wooden figures. "We could have that Father Christmas one – he'd look lovely on the mantelpiece."

Hannah and Olivia were looking at the

stall across the path, full of enormous, stripey lollipops. They both had a little bit of spending money and the lollipops looked like they might last a week, they were so huge.

"Dad, can you ask that lady how much the lollies are?" Hannah glanced back at her parents but they were busy discussing which of the Father Christmases had the nicest face and didn't hear her. "Hey, don't wander off!" She caught Olivia's sleeve. If her little sister went off on her own, they might never find her again. "We'll ask them again in a minute. Let's look at the figures. I think Mum's going to buy one."

Olivia muttered something grumpy about wanting a lollipop now but Hannah knew she wasn't really hungry. They were both full of hot chocolate and the rich spiced gingerbread Dad had bought.

"They're beautiful," Hannah breathed, coming to stand next to Mum. The stall was packed with shelves and shelves of shining figures. Elves, dancers, fairies, tin soldiers and the funniest little carved animals. Hannah smiled at one small cat that looked just like their tabby cat, Misty.

"Aren't they? It's so hard to decide. Some of them are puppets, girls, can you see? The ones hanging up there – they have strings."

Hannah nodded, peering up at the puppets dangling from the ceiling. There was a gorgeous angel puppet with silver wings but she couldn't read the price on the little paper ticket hanging from the angel's painted foot. She had a feeling that the puppets might be very expensive. No two were the same, and the painting was so delicate. She leaned sideways to look at the figure behind the angel. She couldn't quite tell what it was, but she thought it was an animal. It definitely had fur.

HOLLY WEBB

Holly Webb started out as a children's book editor and wrote her first series for the publisher she worked for. She has been writing ever since, with over one hundred books to her name. Holly lives in Berkshire, with her husband and three children. Holly's pet cats are always nosying around when she is trying to type on her laptop.

For more information
about Holly Webb visit:

www.holly-webb.com